THIS WALKER BOOK BELONGS TO:

_____

_____

_____

To Claire, with love

First published 2006 by Walker Books Ltd
87 Vauxhall Walk, London SE11 5HJ

This edition published 2007

10 9 8 7 6 5 4 3 2 1

This book has been typeset in Futura T Light

Printed in China

British Library Cataloguing in Publication Data: a catalogue record for
this book is available from the British Library

ISBN: 978-1-4063-0458-9

www.walkerbooks.co.uk

WALKER BOOKS
AND SUBSIDIARIES
LONDON · BOSTON · SYDNEY · AUCKLAND

Silly
Suzy Goose

Petr Horáček

One day Suzy Goose looked around. She was just like everybody else. I wish I could be different, she thought.

If I was
a bat I could hang
upside down and

FLAP

my wings

If I was a toucan
I could make a loud
SQUAWK

If I was a penguin I could slip and

If I was a giraffe I could

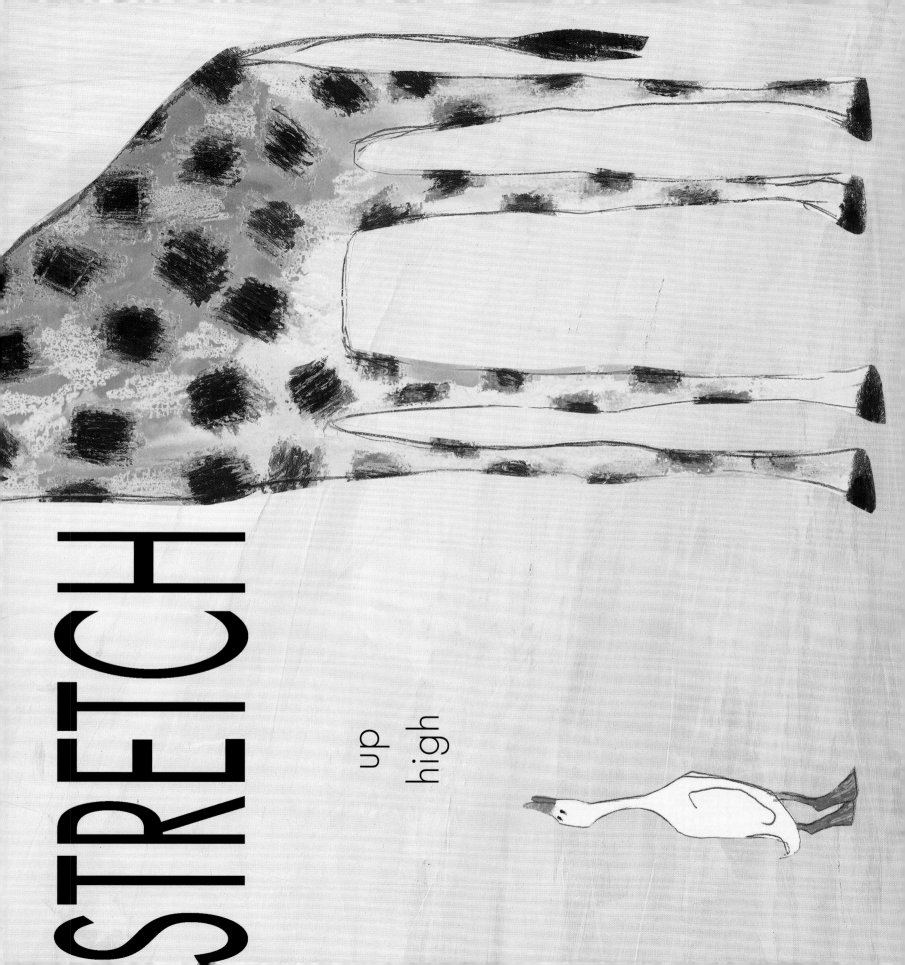

STRETCH

up high

If I was an elephant I could splish and

SPLASH

If I was a kangaroo I could jump, jump, jump, jump and JUMP

If I was an ostrich I could RUN really fast

If I
was a
seal
I could

SWIM

under

the water

If I was a lion I could roar

and **ROAR**

Rroarrhonk!

said Suzy Goose.

But the lion didn't notice.
So Suzy Goose
tried again.
How silly!

This time the lion did notice.

And he didn't like it at all.

Suzy Goose
yelled
and
stretched

and swam

and
jumped

and
splashed

and slid

and flapped
and ran ...

all
the
way
back
to
the
others.

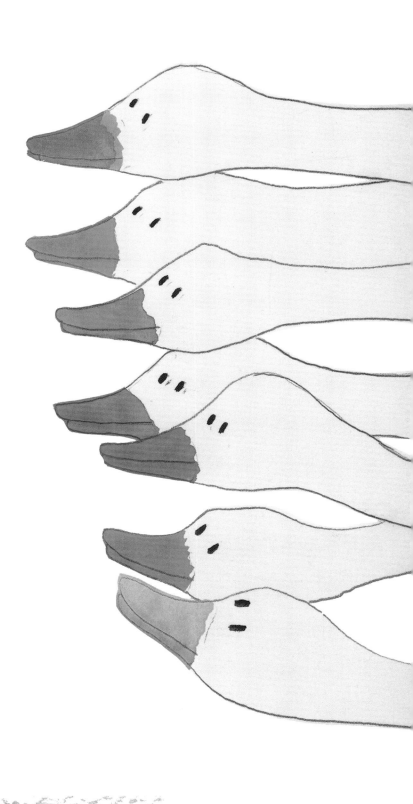

Just in time!

Perhaps it is better to be just like everyone else, thought Suzy Goose ...

but not
all the time.